A Forbidden Visit

The twins got on their bikes and pedaled off. At the end of their block, Jessica turned her bike down Penelope Lane.

"Where are you going?" Elizabeth asked, following close behind. "This isn't the way to the park."

"We're not going to the park. We're going to Ellen's," Jessica said firmly.

"I don't know," Elizabeth said. "We're not supposed to go to friends' houses when no adults are home."

Jessica frowned. "That's just one of the stupid rules Mom and Dad made up because they think we're babies. Anyway, if Debbie and Ellen have fun staying by themselves, they'll have a terrific time with us there."

Elizabeth thought for a minute. Finally she sighed. "All right, I give up. Let's go."

SWEET VALLEY KIDS

ELLEN IS HOME ALONE

Written by
Molly Mia Stewart

Created by
FRANCINE PASCAL

Illustrated by
Ying-Hwa Hu

A BANTAM SKYLARK BOOK®
NEW YORK • TORONTO • LONDON • SYDNEY • AUCKLAND

RL 2, 005–008

ELLEN IS HOME ALONE
A Bantam Skylark Book / May 1993

*Sweet Valley High® and Sweet Valley Kids are trademarks of
Francine Pascal*

Conceived by Francine Pascal

*Produced by Daniel Weiss Associates, Inc.
33 West 17th Street
New York, NY 10011*

Cover art by Susan Tang

*Skylark Books is a registered trademark of Bantam Books, a division
of Bantam Doubleday Dell Publishing Group, Inc. Registered in U.S.
Patent and Trademark Office and elsewhere.*

ISBN 0-553-48013-8

Published simultaneously in the United States and Canada

*Bantam Books are published by Bantam Books, a division of Bantam
Doubleday Dell Publishing Group, Inc. Its trademark, consisting of the
words "Bantam Books" and the portrayal of a rooster, is Registered in
U.S. Patent and Trademark Office and in other countries. Marca Regis-
trada. Bantam Books, 1540 Broadway, New York, New York 10036.*

PRINTED IN THE UNITED STATES OF AMERICA

0 9 8 7 6 5 4 3 2 1

ELLEN
IS
HOME
ALONE

CHAPTER 1

The New Job

"All right!" Jessica Wakefield exclaimed. She rushed out of Sweet Valley Elementary School. "I thought the day would never end."

Her twin sister, Elizabeth Wakefield, shook her head. "That's because you're excited about going to Ellen's house."

"I'm really glad you're coming," Ellen Riteman spoke up. "But the day didn't seem that long to me."

"Me neither. It went by fast—like a race car," Elizabeth agreed.

"Well, not for me," Jessica said, putting her hands on her hips. "It seemed like forever until now. Spelling was especially boring."

Elizabeth and Ellen giggled. "I always love spelling," Elizabeth said.

Jessica groaned.

"I can't believe you two are twins," Ellen said.

It was true. Elizabeth and Jessica were different in many ways. Elizabeth liked reading and making up stories, and she enjoyed all of her classes at school. She was a proud member of the Sweet Valley Soccer League and loved to play outside, even if it meant getting dirty.

Jessica hated to mess up her clothes. In fact, she didn't like playing outdoors at all. She preferred to stay inside and play with

her dolls and stuffed animals. The only reason she liked going to school was that she got to talk and play with all her friends there.

But Jessica and Elizabeth had a lot in common, too. They were identical twins, which meant that they looked exactly the same. They both had blue-green eyes and long blond hair with bangs. When they wore identical outfits to school, only their best friends could tell them apart. That's why each wore a name bracelet.

"Where is your mom picking us up?" Jessica asked.

"Right here in front of school," Ellen said, putting down her bag.

Ellen was in the twins' class. She had brown hair that she'd just gotten cut into a chin-length bob. Her blue eyes were framed by thick brown lashes. Ellen was pretty, but she wasn't as sweet as she looked. She loved to tease and make fun of kids she didn't like, and she could be a bit snobby. Once she, Jessica, and their friend Lila Fowler had even started a club that nobody else was allowed to join.

Elizabeth didn't like the way Ellen sometimes teased kids, like Andy Franklin and Lois Waller. But most of the time Ellen was nice, and she was fun to play with. So even though Ellen was mostly Jessica's friend, both twins were going to Ellen's house to play that afternoon.

Jessica and Elizabeth sat down on the steps outside the school to wait for Mrs. Riteman. Ellen walked along a low wall that ran outside the school driveway. She held out her arms and balanced like a gymnast.

A girl with straight brown hair sneaked up behind Ellen. She turned to the twins and put a finger to her lips. She gave Ellen a push. Ellen fell off the wall and landed on her feet. She wasn't hurt, but she was angry.

"Hey," Ellen yelled, turning around. "Cut it out."

The other girl rolled her eyes. "What a baby."

"Is that Ellen's sister?" Elizabeth whispered to Jessica.

Jessica nodded. "Her name's Debbie."

"She reminds me of Steven," Elizabeth said. Steven was the twins' older brother. He could be a real pain in the neck sometimes.

"Debbie's worse," Jessica said.

Elizabeth shook her head. "Impossible."

A cream-colored station wagon pulled up.

Mrs. Riteman was behind the wheel. She beeped the horn.

Debbie turned toward Jessica and Elizabeth and crossed her arms over her chest. "I always sit in the front seat. Alone. Give me any trouble, and you'll be sorry."

Jessica looked at Elizabeth and rolled her eyes. "See, nothing's impossible."

"Debbie always wants things her way," Ellen told them. "I don't argue with her. It's not worth it." Ellen climbed into the backseat of the car. Her four-year-old brother, Mark, was already strapped in. Dixon, the Ritemans' dog, was sitting in the large wagon area.

"Hi, boy," Elizabeth said as she and Jessica squeezed in next to Ellen. "I love dogs."

"And Dixon loves children," Mrs. Riteman said. "It's nice to see you girls."

"Hello, Mrs. Riteman," Elizabeth and Jessica said as the car started to move. Dixon immediately jumped over the seat and landed on Elizabeth's lap.

Elizabeth giggled. But Jessica yelped. She was afraid of dogs. "Get him away from me. Please!" Jessica said, pressing up against Ellen.

Debbie turned around. "Don't send him up here. I don't want to get fur on my clothes."

Elizabeth helped Ellen push Dixon into the back again. She thought that Debbie was being really bossy. She was glad that Debbie wasn't *her* sister.

When they arrived at the Ritemans' house, Mrs. Riteman poured five glasses of milk and set a huge plate of chocolate peanut butter chip cookies on the kitchen table.

No one said anything for a while as they ate and drank.

"Did you hear about your job?" Ellen finally asked her mother.

Mrs. Riteman smiled. "I'm glad you asked. The Sweet Valley Museum called this morning and offered me the fund-raising job I told you about."

Debbie's eyes widened. "Did you take it?"

"I sure did," Mrs. Riteman said. "I'm very excited."

Jessica smiled at Mrs. Riteman. "Congratulations."

Ellen got up and hugged her mom.

"It is great news. But this is going to mean a lot of changes for you kids," Mrs. Riteman continued. "I'm going to have to leave the house by eight thirty every morning."

"That means you won't be able to drive us

to school," Debbie said. "Who's going to take us?"

"You're going to have to take the bus from now on," Mrs. Riteman replied. "Coming home, too."

Debbie frowned. "Disgusting. The bus is slow and crowded."

"What time will you get home?" Ellen asked, taking another cookie.

"Around dinnertime," Mrs. Riteman told her.

"Will I have to baby-sit Mark?" Debbie asked.

"No," Mrs. Riteman said. "For the first few weeks, Stacey or Karen will come over. Then we'll find a permanent baby-sitter."

"When does your job start?" Ellen asked.

"Tomorrow, I'm afraid," Mrs. Riteman

said. "It's a bit sudden. But they need me right away."

Ellen looked at her mother. "I'll miss you."

"I'll miss you, too," Mrs. Riteman said, standing up. "But everything will work out. Now I'm going to call your grandmother and tell her the news."

As soon as Mrs. Riteman left the room, Debbie jumped up. "We have to talk Mom and Dad out of getting a baby-sitter," she said to Ellen. "We're old enough to stay by ourselves."

"That would be great," Jessica agreed. "Only really young kids need a baby-sitter. You've got to prove that you don't need one."

"You don't have much time," Elizabeth pointed out. "Your mom starts work tomorrow."

"We'd better start planning," Debbie said. "Right now."

By the time Mrs. Riteman took the twins home, Debbie and Ellen had their plan ready.

CHAPTER 2

Responsibility

"Action!" Debbie and Ellen yelled as soon as the door closed. The girls knew it would take their mother only a few minutes to drive the twins home.

Debbie made a salad. Ellen set the table. Debbie fed Dixon. Ellen folded a load of laundry.

"We haven't done this many chores in a week," Debbie said.

"Two weeks," Ellen said.

When Mrs. Riteman came home and walked into the kitchen, she looked impressed. "Thanks for being such a big help," she told them.

Debbie smiled. "Since you're going to be busy with work now, we want to help out more. Anything you need done, just tell us."

Ellen bit her lip. Debbie was going a bit far. What if their mother decided she wanted the basement cleaned? They'd be down there for weeks. And Ellen hated the basement—it was dark and scary.

Mrs. Riteman chuckled. "Thanks, girls. I'll certainly keep that in mind. But I think you've done enough for today."

"Hello," Mr. Riteman called out from the front hall. "I'm home!"

"Hi, Dad," Debbie said, running to her father. She took his briefcase. "I'll put this in the closet."

"Would you like me to get your slippers?" Ellen asked.

"No, thanks." Mr. Riteman looked puzzled. "What's going on?"

"Nothing," Mrs. Riteman told him, giving him a kiss. "The girls are just in a helpful mood. They practically cooked dinner by themselves."

Mr. Riteman pulled out his chair. "I thought you said nothing was going on," he said with a laugh.

"I do have some news," Mrs. Riteman said. She sat down and told Mr. Riteman about her new job.

"That's wonderful!" he exclaimed, looking happy and proud. "Did you find a sitter for tomorrow?"

"No," Mrs. Riteman said. "Karen and Stacey are both busy."

15

Debbie cleared her throat. "I have an idea. Why don't Ellen and I stay alone? I'm already nine. That's too old to need a babysitter."

"Remember last weekend?" Ellen asked. "Debbie and I stayed by ourselves, and nothing bad happened."

"That was only for a few hours," Mrs. Riteman said.

"But it would only be a few hours every afternoon," Debbie pointed out. "It's no different."

Mr. and Mrs. Riteman exchanged a look. "Your father and I need some time to talk things over," Mrs. Riteman said. "I hadn't thought about this possibility at all."

"Ellen and I would be fine alone," Debbie said. "I promise we'd be good."

Ellen nodded. "We'd be angels."

*   *   *

"Girls! Would you come in here, please?"

It was just before bedtime. Debbie and Ellen had been watching their favorite show on television. But they jumped up and ran into the kitchen when their mother called.

"Did you decide?" Debbie demanded, looking from her mother to her father.

Mr. Riteman nodded and held out two house keys on metal chains. "We think you girls can stay home alone."

"All right!" Ellen yelled.

"Awesome," Debbie shouted. "You won't be sorry."

Ellen and Debbie exchanged high fives.

"Shh," Mrs. Riteman said. "Your brother is sleeping."

"I forgot all about Mark," Debbie said. "What are you going to do with him?"

18

"Your brother will go to day care," Mrs. Riteman said. "A lot of the kids from his play group go, so I think he'll have a good time. I'll pick him up on the way home from work."

"We're letting you stay by yourselves because we think we can trust you," Mr. Riteman said. "But we want you to know that more independence means more responsibility."

"Since you girls get the *independence* of staying home," Mrs. Riteman said, "you also have the *responsibility* of some extra jobs around the house."

"No problem," Ellen said. "We'll do whatever you say."

Mrs. Riteman got up and walked over to the refrigerator. "Come look at this, then," she said, pointing to a long piece of paper held on the refrigerator door by an elephant magnet. On the paper was a list of important phone numbers: Mr. and Mrs. Riteman at work, the girls' grandparents, the police and fire departments, the plumber, and several of the Ritemans' neighbors.

"I called Mrs. Keller," Mrs. Riteman told Ellen and Debbie. Mrs. Keller was a friendly neighbor who lived a few doors down from the Ritemans. "She said she'd be happy to keep an eye on you."

Debbie frowned. "I thought we weren't going to have a baby-sitter."

"Mrs. Keller isn't going to be baby-sitting you," Mrs. Riteman explained. "But in case anything happens, she's close by. You can call her if you need to."

Mr. Riteman then took the girls down to the basement. He showed them the circuit breakers and the water main. He always gave baby-sitters the same tour, so Ellen had heard it dozens of times before.

But this time there isn't a baby-sitter, Ellen thought. *Just me and Debbie.* She bit her thumbnail.

"Isn't this outrageous?" Debbie whispered. "I'm so happy I thought of it."

"It's unbelievable," Ellen said. She didn't tell her sister that she was starting to get a little bit nervous.

CHAPTER 3

Babies No More

"My mom is starting a new job today," Ellen announced during show-and-tell the next day. "My sister, Debbie, and I are going to stay home by ourselves every afternoon until dinnertime without a baby-sitter."

"Wow," Todd Wilkins said. "My parents would never let me do that."

Ellen smiled. She was the only second grader so far to be allowed to stay home alone. "This is my house key." She pulled a key out from under her T-shirt and held it up so everyone in the class could see. "I'm going to use it to let myself into the house. Today will be the first time."

"Be careful, so you don't lose it," said Mrs. Otis, the teacher. "You don't want to get locked out."

"I won't," Ellen said. "I'm never going to take it off. I slept with it last night."

"Good. You're behaving very responsibly," Mrs. Otis said.

"Can you believe it?" Lila whispered to Jessica.

Jessica shook her head. "I wish I were allowed to stay home alone."

"I'm so jealous," Eva Simpson told Ellen at lunch. "My parents don't ever leave me alone in the house."

Jessica sighed. Ellen had been the center

of attention all morning. Now lots of kids were gathered around her at the lunch table.

"Are you excited?" Lila asked.

"Definitely," Ellen said. "I'm going to eat ice cream for a snack every day. And I'm going to jump on my bed. And Debbie and I are going to watch hours of TV while my parents are at work. It'll be great. I can't wait."

"I wish our parents would leave us alone sometimes," Jessica told Elizabeth.

Elizabeth smiled. "I'm not so sure. Steven would really be bossy."

"I can handle Steven," Jessica said. "And anyway, don't you think Mom and Dad treat us like babies?"

Elizabeth thought for a minute. "Sometimes."

"I think it's time to make them stop," Jessica decided.

*　　*　　*

That afternoon, Mrs. Wakefield took the twins shopping downtown. One of Mrs. Wakefield's friends was getting married, and the twins needed new dresses to wear to the wedding.

"Give me your hands while we cross the street," Mrs. Wakefield told Jessica and Elizabeth.

Jessica hid hers behind her back. "I can cross the street by myself."

"We're not babies anymore," Elizabeth added.

"I know that," Mrs. Wakefield said, looking surprised. "But Vine Street is dangerous. I wouldn't want anything to happen to you." She took the girls' hands. After they crossed the street, she let go.

Jessica and Elizabeth ran ahead to the

store. "It's closed," they told their mother when she caught up to them.

Mrs. Wakefield sighed. "I guess we'll have to come back another day." She reached down and took Elizabeth's left hand and Jessica's right one. "Here we go again."

Jessica frowned. *Ellen is lucky,* she told herself. *Her mother trusts her. My mother treats me and Elizabeth like babies.*

She stomped across the street. She was imagining all the fun Debbie and Ellen were having by themselves.

CHAPTER 4

Ice Cream and Cartoons

"I'm going to beat you there," Ellen yelled. She was running as fast as she could.

"No, you're not," Debbie called, passing Ellen and running up to the front door. She hurried to pull out her house key.

Ellen already had her key out. Each of the girls wanted to be the first to use her new key. Ellen tried to slide hers into the keyhole first. But her sister was too fast. Debbie jammed her key in the lock and turned it.

Ellen frowned. "I'll win tomorrow."

"You'll never win," Debbie said. "My legs are longer."

"Just wait," Ellen said.

As Debbie and Ellen walked inside, they both fell quiet. Their voices sounded too loud in the empty house. Everything was so still that Ellen felt like tiptoeing. Goose bumps formed on her arms.

Debbie went into the kitchen. Ellen stayed close behind her, not wanting to be left all alone anywhere in the big empty house. "Look," Debbie said, opening the refrigerator. "Mom left us a snack." She pointed to a plate of carrot sticks and tuna sandwiches. "Yuck!"

"And look at this," Ellen said. She picked up a piece of paper from the countertop. "Here's a list of chores. I'm supposed to clean four potatoes for dinner. You're supposed to vacuum the first floor."

"More independence means more responsibility," Debbie said, mimicking her father. She stuck out her tongue. "What a drag."

Ellen nodded. Then she tilted her head and turned around. "What was that?"

Debbie shrugged. "What was what?"

Ellen stood still and listened. But the only sounds she heard were coming from behind her, where Debbie was taking a gallon of ice cream out of the freezer. Ellen's mouth dropped open. She forgot about the noise. "But Mom said—"

"Mom isn't here," Debbie interrupted, pulling a spoon out of a drawer and digging some ice cream out of the box.

"Dad will notice it's gone," Ellen pointed out.

"Get real," Debbie said. "You know as well as I do that Dad is an ice cream freak. The freezer is crammed full of the stuff. He'll never notice if a little is missing."

Ellen hesitated.

"It's vanilla fudge twirl," Debbie said. "Your favorite. Anyway, you told me you'd have ice cream for a snack every afternoon now that Mom is working. Are you chickening out?"

Ellen shook her head. "No. Let's eat it in front of the TV. Give me four *big* scoops."

She and Debbie sat on the den couch with bowls full of ice cream. They kept the gallon box between them. By the time they had watched TV for an hour, they had finished the entire gallon. Soon a game show came on.

Ellen hated game shows, but she didn't

move. Mr. and Mrs. Riteman never let the girls watch more than an hour of television a day. Now Ellen and Debbie could watch all they wanted. Ellen wanted to watch a lot. But there was another reason why she wasn't moving.

"I feel sick," Ellen said.

Debbie closed her eyes and groaned. "Me too. I couldn't eat another spoonful."

Just then they heard the front door open. "Girls," Mrs. Riteman called out. "I'm home. I brought dinner!"

Ellen and Debbie jumped up. Debbie ran to turn off the TV, while Ellen shoved the empty ice-cream box under the couch.

Debbie hurried out to the front hall. "Hi, Mom," Ellen heard her sister say. "I'm so glad you're home. Ellen and I are starving."

CHAPTER 5

Breaking the Rules

"Did you have fun yesterday?" Elizabeth asked Ellen the next day after school. They were on the bus home.

Ellen smiled. "Debbie and I ate an entire gallon of ice cream."

"Really?" Jessica said. "I've never had that much at one time."

"It was great," Ellen said. "But right after we finished the ice cream, my mother came home. We had to pretend to be hungry for dinner—and then we had to eat everything."

"Did you turn green?" Elizabeth asked, wide-eyed.

Ellen nodded. "That's not even the worst part. My dad brought home a chocolate cake for dessert."

The twins groaned.

"Did you eat any?" Elizabeth asked.

"A big piece," Ellen said. "I had to. My parents know I love chocolate cake. They would have known something was up if I hadn't eaten any. Debbie fed hers to Dixon under the table."

The bus stopped. Debbie walked by and hit Ellen on the head. "Come on, Shrimp. I'm starving."

"Is it our stop already?" Ellen asked. She grabbed her backpack and ran after her sister. "See you guys tomorrow."

"It sounds like Debbie and Ellen are having a lot of fun," Elizabeth said.

"I know," Jessica said. She didn't sound happy about it.

A few minutes later, Elizabeth, Jessica, and Steven climbed off the bus. Mrs. Wakefield was waiting for them when they got home.

"How was your day?" she asked as they walked into the kitchen.

"You ask us that question every afternoon," Elizabeth said.

"Not on Saturdays," Mrs. Wakefield said.

Steven laughed. "Or Sundays."

"Very funny," Elizabeth said.

Steven opened the refrigerator. "What can we eat?"

"I made you some fruit salad," Mrs. Wakefield said.

"Fruit salad?" Jessica asked. "Can't we pick our own snacks?"

Mrs. Wakefield smiled as she shook her head. "I don't want you eating only junk food all the time."

"I'd pick chocolate cake smothered with marshmallow fluff," Steven said.

Mrs. Wakefield made a face. "See what I mean?"

Jessica popped a piece of apple into her mouth. "Can Liz and I go to the park after we finish eating?"

"Sure," Mrs. Wakefield said. "Just remember to be careful and look both ways when you cross the street."

A few minutes later, the twins got on their bikes and pedaled off. But at the end of their block, Jessica turned her bike down Penelope Lane.

"Where are you going?" Elizabeth asked, following close behind. "This isn't the way to the park."

"We're not going to the park. We're going to Ellen's," Jessica said firmly.

"What? Why?" Elizabeth asked.

"To get a *real* snack," Jessica answered.

"I don't know." Elizabeth caught up to her sister's side. "We're not supposed to go to friends' houses when no adults are home."

Jessica frowned. "That's just one of the stupid rules Mom and Dad made up because they think we're babies."

"But I told Amy I'd meet her at the park," Elizabeth said.

"Look at it this way," Jessica said. "If Debbie and Ellen have fun staying by themselves, they'll have a terrific time with us there."

Elizabeth thought for a minute. She didn't like disobeying her parents, but Jessica's argument made sense. Some of Mr. and Mrs. Wakefield's rules *were* too babyish. Finally she sighed. "All right, I give up. Let's go."

CHAPTER 6

A Burglar

Ellen kicked the leg of the couch and stared at the TV. "I'm so bored," she groaned. "These game shows are so stupid."

Just then, the doorbell rang.

"Get it," Debbie ordered.

"I'm watching TV," Ellen said. "You get it. You're not doing anything."

Debbie leaned over Ellen. "Don't forget. I'm bigger than you are. So get it or else!"

Ellen sighed. She got up and stomped to the front door. But she perked up when she saw Jessica and Elizabeth standing outside.

"Hi, you guys," she said. "What are you doing here?"

"We came for some ice cream," Jessica explained. "It sounded so good when you talked about it today."

"Okay," Ellen said. "Come into the kitchen."

"I don't think we have time for ice cream," Elizabeth said, going into the house. "We just wanted to say hi."

"We're not supposed to be here," Jessica said. "Elizabeth's afraid of getting into trouble."

"Aren't you afraid, Jessica?" Debbie asked, walking into the kitchen.

"Nope," Jessica said. "Breaking one of Mom and Dad's baby rules makes coming over here even more fun."

Ellen put two bowls on the table.

"I'll have some ice cream, too," Debbie said. She walked to the freezer and pulled out a box.

"Really?" Ellen said. "I'm not going to eat ice cream for a month."

Suddenly, Ellen froze. She heard a noise. It was the same noise she had heard the day before. Her heart started beating faster. She wished her mother were there. Staying home alone was scary.

"What's the matter?" Elizabeth asked.

"Shh!" Ellen ordered. "Don't you hear that?"

"I don't hear anything," Jessica said.

"Listen," Ellen hissed.

And then there was a loud—*bang*!

"I heard *that*," Elizabeth said.

Now Debbie looked alarmed. "It's coming from the front porch."

"That's not the sound I meant," Ellen said.

Bang!

Elizabeth's eyes widened. "I think someone is trying to get into the house."

"You mean a—a burglar?" Jessica said, her voice quavering.

Bang!

"We have to call the police," Ellen whispered. She ran to the phone and dialed 911.

Elizabeth, Jessica, and Debbie listened to the lock of the front door turning.

"It's ringing," Ellen whispered. "Please answer fast."

The door swung open. The burglar was in the house.

"Debbie! Ellen! Where are you?" It was Mr. Riteman calling from the hall.

The twins exchanged worried looks. Ellen slammed down the phone.

"Hi, Daddy," Debbie called out. She ran into the hall and blocked her father's path into the kitchen.

Ellen threw the ice cream back into the freezer. She stacked up the bowls and put them into a cupboard. "He's a whole hour early," Ellen whispered. "You guys better go."

"Come on, Liz," Jessica said, grabbing Elizabeth's hand and heading for the kitchen door. "Let's get out of here."

CHAPTER 7

Bedtime Blues

That evening, Jessica and Elizabeth were watching television with their father.

"Don't touch that dial—*The Bryant Files* is next," Jessica said from her place on the den floor.

Mr. Wakefield stood up and stretched. "Come on, you two. It's time for bed."

"Please," Elizabeth said. "We really want to watch *The Bryant Files* tonight."

Mr. Wakefield shook his head. "You know you're not allowed to watch that cops-and-robbers show. It's too grown-up for you. Besides, it doesn't end until an hour after your bedtime—which, by the way, is exactly this minute."

Jessica and Elizabeth didn't move.

"Okay, troops," Mr. Wakefield yelled. "Fall in!"

The twins still didn't move.

Mr. Wakefield picked up the remote control. He flicked off the television.

Jessica and Elizabeth groaned.

"At least I got your attention," Mr. Wakefield said. "Come on. It's time for you to hit the hay."

"But we're not tired," Jessica complained. "I won't be able to fall asleep for hours."

Elizabeth yawned.

Mr. Wakefield smiled. "I know *you're* not tired. I'm putting you to bed because *I'm* exhausted."

Slowly, Jessica and Elizabeth got up and walked into the kitchen. Mrs. Wakefield was sitting at the table, helping Steven with his math homework.

"Good night, Jessica," Mrs. Wakefield said. "Good night, Elizabeth."

The twins kissed their mother, then followed Mr. Wakefield upstairs.

"What do you want to hear for your bedtime story?" Mr. Wakefield asked after Jessica and Elizabeth had brushed their teeth and changed into their pajamas.

"Nothing," Elizabeth said. She had already climbed into bed. "We know how to read to ourselves."

"I know," Mr. Wakefield said, frowning. "But does this mean I'm never going to get to read *Green Eggs and Ham* again?"

Jessica giggled. "You can borrow it any time you want."

Mr. Wakefield smiled. "That's a relief."

Elizabeth rolled her eyes. "Good night, Dad."

"I'm not leaving without my good-night kisses," Mr. Wakefield insisted.

Jessica and Elizabeth kissed their father good night. Then Mr. Wakefield turned out the overhead light and turned on the night-light.

"We don't need that," Jessica said. "We're not afraid of the dark."

Mr. Wakefield raised an eyebrow. "No night-light?"

"Nope!" Jessica said.

Mr. Wakefield turned it off.

"Please close the door too," Elizabeth told him.

Mr. Wakefield looked surprised. "Are you sure?"

"Yes," Jessica said, looking at her sister. "Right, Liz?"

"Right," Elizabeth said.

"Okay. Sleep well." Mr. Wakefield shut the door behind him.

The room was suddenly pitch black. "Good night, Liz," Jessica said.

"Good night, Jess," Elizabeth whispered.

Elizabeth's eyes were wide open. She couldn't see a thing, but she could hear the tree branches rustling in the wind outside. Then, as her eyes adjusted to the dark, she saw shadows moving across the wall. They looked like monsters.

"Jessica," she said softly. "Are you awake?"

There was no answer, just a steady

breathing coming from the other bed. Elizabeth knew Jessica was sound asleep. So she crawled out of bed and turned on the nightlight. Next she opened the door. Only then did Elizabeth climb back into bed and fall into a deep sleep.

CHAPTER 8

Cinder-Ellen

"Do you need help washing the blackboards?" Ellen asked Mrs. Otis as school ended the next day.

"No, thanks," Mrs. Otis said. "You don't have time to wash them, anyway. You have to catch the bus. Remember?"

Ellen remembered. But she had been hoping that Mrs. Otis would forget until it was too late. Ellen picked up her backpack. "Okay, see you tomorrow."

She walked to the bus slowly. For the first time that week, she didn't want to go home.

Ever since she'd heard the noise no one else heard, Ellen had been worried. She wished she were going home to her mother instead of to an empty house full of scary sounds. She considered calling her mother at the museum and telling her that she was sick. But then Ellen would be stuck in bed for days. She decided that the only thing to do was to convince Debbie that the noise was something to take seriously. She knew it wasn't going to be easy, though.

"I want to talk to you about something," Ellen told Debbie as they were walking home from the bus stop.

"I want to talk to you, too," Debbie said. "I'll go first."

Ellen felt hopeful. Maybe Debbie finally believed that there was a strange noise coming from somewhere in the house. Maybe Debbie was scared too.

"From now on, you have to do all of my afternoon chores," Debbie announced. "*And* clean my room."

Ellen laughed. "Why would I do that?"

"Because if you don't," Debbie said, "I'll tell Mom and Dad that Jessica and Elizabeth came over yesterday."

"You can't tell," Ellen said. "Mom and Dad would freak out. And Jessica and Elizabeth would get in big trouble."

"I won't tell," Debbie said. "As long as you do what I tell you to."

Ellen frowned. Sometimes she couldn't believe how mean her sister was. Ellen didn't understand how they could be related.

Debbie opened their front door. "I don't

think you should watch any TV today. Mom sounded really serious last night."

The evening before, Mrs. Riteman had told the girls she noticed that they hadn't been doing their afternoon chores. She had ordered them to shape up—or else.

"I don't want to watch TV, anyway," Ellen said. She stomped into the kitchen and glanced at the list of chores her mother had posted on the refrigerator. The table had to be set. That was Ellen's responsibility. And Debbie was supposed to make a salad. Now Ellen had to do both.

"I feel like Cinder-Ellen," she muttered. "That makes Debbie my evil stepsister. I hope she grows a wart on her nose."

Ellen banged open the refrigerator and pulled out the carrots. She was making as much noise as she could. She wanted to bother Debbie, but the television was blaring so loudly in the other room that Ellen was sure her sister couldn't hear a thing. Ellen slammed the refrigerator door closed.

Suddenly, her heart skipped a beat. She thought she had heard the noise again. No, she *knew* she had heard it. It was louder. Much louder.

Ellen ran into the other room. "I heard it again!"

"Heard what?" Debbie asked.

"The noise," Ellen whispered, close to tears. "I'm afraid."

"Would you forget about that stupid noise?" Debbie said, putting her feet up on the couch. "Look what happened last time. You almost called the police over nothing."

Ellen's mouth fell open. "You're so mean!" she yelled. "I wish you weren't my sister!"

CHAPTER 9

A Dangerous Crossing

"I hope we have better luck today," Mrs. Wakefield said. She pulled the car into a parking spot. She was taking the twins back to the same shop that had been closed a few days earlier. "The wedding is in just one week," she added.

Elizabeth jumped out of the car. Jessica was right behind her.

"Wait for me on the curb," Mrs. Wakefield called out.

Jessica and Elizabeth stopped. They watched the traffic zoom by.

"There are tons of cars on this street," Elizabeth said.

"They really go fast," Jessica added.

"Okay, let me have your hands," Mrs. Wakefield said when she got to the curb. Elizabeth and Jessica looked at each other and frowned.

When the light changed, the three of them walked across the street holding hands. Jessica and Elizabeth broke free as soon as they reached the other side. Jessica ran up to the store.

"It's open," she announced.

Mrs. Wakefield led the way inside. "Why don't you two see if you can find anything you like?"

"Great," Jessica said. She loved to shop. "Come on, Liz."

A few minutes later, Jessica ran up to her

mother. She was carrying a pink dress with long sleeves.

"How about this one?" Jessica asked. "It's fancy."

Mrs. Wakefield looked at the dress. "It is fancy, honey. But the wedding is going to be outside. I think you'd be too hot in that."

"I don't think so," Jessica protested. "It's the only dress I want."

"Jessica, be reasonable," Mrs. Wakefield said. She held up a pretty peach-colored dress with embroidery on the front. "This is just as nice and much more appropriate."

Jessica wrinkled her nose. "It looks like something a kindergartener would wear."

Elizabeth came up to them. She was holding a yellow jumper. "Do you like this one, Jess?"

Jessica nodded. "It's pretty."

"That does look perfect for a wedding," Mrs. Wakefield agreed. But the store didn't have the jumper in the twins' size.

"I'm sorry," the saleswoman said. "And I'm afraid you'll have to make your purchases right away. We'll be closing in five minutes."

Mrs. Wakefield sighed. "I guess we'll have to get the peach one."

"No!" Jessica yelled. "I want the pink one!"

"Jessica, you're too young to choose all of your own clothes," Mrs. Wakefield said. "I'm afraid I have to make this decision."

"I am not too young to pick my clothes!" Jessica shouted. "That's just one of your stupid rules."

"What's gotten into you, Jessica?" Mrs. Wakefield asked. "Rules aren't stupid."

"The one about not going to a friend's

house when their parents aren't home is," Jessica said. "Liz and I went to Ellen's yesterday, and nothing bad happened."

Mrs. Wakefield looked very surprised. "You did that?" She shook her head. "I'm very disappointed in you, Jessica. And you, too, Elizabeth."

Jessica stomped her foot. "Stop treating us like babies!"

"That's exactly what you're acting like," Mrs. Wakefield said quietly. "Now, let's just go home."

"No!" Jessica turned and ran out of the store. She stopped for a second on the sidewalk to look both ways and then ran straight across Vine Street.

"Jessica, wait!" Elizabeth yelled, running after her. She ran into the street without looking. When she did look to the left, she

saw a car headed right for her. Elizabeth froze.

The car slammed on its brakes and started to skid. At the last second, Mrs. Wakefield, who had run out of the store after the twins, grabbed Elizabeth and pulled her across the street out of danger.

Elizabeth was sobbing. So was Jessica.

Mrs. Wakefield gave them each a hug. "Are you two okay?"

Jessica and Elizabeth nodded.

"I'm so glad," Mrs. Wakefield said. She brushed the hair out of the twins' eyes and gave them each another hug.

Then Mrs. Wakefield sat back on her heels. "Jessica, that was a stupid thing to do. You could have been killed. And Elizabeth, you ran right into the street without looking."

"I'm sorry, Mom," Elizabeth said, wiping away her tears.

"Me, too," Jessica said.

"I know you both are growing up," Mrs. Wakefield said. "But part of growing up is knowing which rules are the most important."

"Like not crossing a busy street by yourself," Elizabeth said.

"And not going over to a friend's when their parents aren't home," Jessica added quietly.

Mrs. Wakefield smiled. "Yes. Those are both important rules." She thought for a minute. "But I agree that you're old enough to pick your own clothes. So what do you say we go to the mall and see if we can find something there?"

Jessica smiled. "All right!"

CHAPTER 10

Brave Ellen

Ellen tiptoed into the kitchen. Her heart was pounding. She stopped to listen and decided the noise was coming from the basement. Spiders lived down there. Ellen thought there might be mice, too. Maybe even bats or rats.

Taking a deep breath, Ellen put her hand on the basement doorknob and turned it. The noise was much louder. Still, she walked down two steps. And then she saw it —water everywhere.

Water was dripping slowly from a pipe

near the ceiling. The basement was flooded. Ellen figured the pipe must have been dripping for days. *That was the noise I heard,* Ellen told herself. She was so relieved that she laughed out loud.

Ellen quickly turned off the water main, just as her parents had taught her. She ran upstairs and called the plumber. Then she called her mother, who got home fifteen minutes later.

"Girls, where are you?" Mrs. Riteman yelled.

"Down here," Ellen called up the basement steps.

Mrs. Riteman came down. She looked around and smiled. "I see that everything is under control. I'm so impressed with you. You're even more grown-up than I thought. Thank you both."

Debbie leaned on her mop handle. "Don't thank me. Ellen did everything."

Ellen smiled. "Debbie helped me mop up."

The doorbell rang. "I bet that's the plumber," Mrs. Riteman said. She ran up the stairs.

"I still can't believe you came down here by yourself," Debbie told Ellen.

Ellen smiled. "Why would I be afraid of a little noise?"

At school the next day, Ellen told everyone what had happened.

"Debbie is a lot nicer to me now," she said to Jessica and Elizabeth. "I bet it won't last, though."

"Yeah, but take advantage of it while you can," Jessica said. "Dad told us our cousins Robin and Stacey are coming to visit. Stacey is younger, but Robin is seven, too. Steven will probably boss us all around."

"At least Robin is fun," Elizabeth said. "She plays soccer."

"And she likes dolls," Jessica added.

Ellen looked from one twin to the other. "Robin will have a hard time choosing who to play with."

"She'll play with both of us," Elizabeth said.

Jessica nodded. "Right. Robin will have the best time. And so will we."

Will Jessica and Elizabeth get along with their cousin when she comes to visit? Find out in Sweet Valley Kids #40, **ROBIN IN THE MIDDLE.**

SWEET VALLEY KIDS

Jessica and Elizabeth have had lots of adventures in *Sweet Valley High* and *Sweet Valley Twins*...now read about the twins at age seven! You'll love all the fun that comes with being seven—birthday parties, playing dress-up, class projects, putting on puppet shows and plays, losing a tooth, setting up lemonade stands, caring for animals and much more! It's all part of SWEET VALLEY KIDS. Read them all!

- [ ] **JESSICA AND THE SPELLING-BEE SURPRISE #21**   15917-8 $2.75
- [ ] **SWEET VALLEY SLUMBER PARTY #22**   15934-8 $2.99
- [ ] **LILA'S HAUNTED HOUSE PARTY # 23**   15919-4 $2.99
- [ ] **COUSIN KELLY'S FAMILY SECRET # 24**   15920-8 $2.99
- [ ] **LEFT-OUT ELIZABETH # 25**   15921-6 $2.99
- [ ] **JESSICA'S SNOBBY CLUB # 26**   15922-4 $2.99
- [ ] **THE SWEET VALLEY CLEANUP TEAM # 27**   15923-2 $2.99
- [ ] **ELIZABETH MEETS HER HERO #28**   15924-0 $2.99
- [ ] **ANDY AND THE ALIEN # 29**   15925-9 $2.99
- [ ] **JESSICA'S UNBURIED TREASURE # 30**   15926-7 $2.99
- [ ] **ELIZABETH AND JESSICA RUN AWAY # 31**   48004-9 $2.99
- [ ] **LEFT BACK! #32**   48005-7 $2.99
- [ ] **CAROLINE'S HALLOWEEN SPELL # 33**   48006-5 $2.99
- [ ] **THE BEST THANKSGIVING EVER # 34**   48007-3 $2.99
- [ ] **ELIZABETH'S BROKEN ARM # 35**   48009-X $2.99
- [ ] **ELIZABETH'S VIDEO FEVER # 36**   48010-3 $2.99
- [ ] **THE BIG RACE # 37**   48011-1 $2.99